Contents

1

Edek at School

Edek hated his new school.
It was no better than the old one.
As each day passed, it was worse.
He hated it more than
anything else in his life.

In every lesson, he had the same problems.
'He's such a pain,' they said loudly.
'We don't want him in our group.
No way,' they sneered.
'Tell him to get lost.
He's pathetic,' they jeered.

Edek hated having to see the teachers.

'Tell us what happened, Edek,' they'd say.
There was always a long silence.

He felt so stupid.
He couldn't get any words out of his mouth.
They stuck in his throat.
The web of thin skin between
his fingers itched.
His body felt hot and dry.
Why did it always have to be like this?

The teachers would talk about him
behind his back.

'He's a weird kid,' they'd say.
'Have you ever seen such cold eyes?
Such strange, blue eyes.
Eyes like water.'

2

The Operation

When Edek got home, his dad was angry.
'You said you were going to make a effort
in your new school,' he said.
'That's why we let you leave the old one.'

Edek shrank back against the door
of the living room.
His dad was nasty when he was
in one of his moods.

'I've just had a teacher on the phone,'
said his dad.
'They want me to go up to school tomorrow.
I'll have to take the morning off work.
You're causing us hassle again.

'Why do you always do it?
Don't stand there like a lump of jelly.
Answer me, will you?'

Edek looked down at the ground.
His mother saw the sad look on his face.
'Oh Edek,' she said.
'Why are you in such pain?
Can't you tell us what's wrong?'

She remembered the day
she took him to the hospital.
He was going to have an operation.
They were going to cut
the thin web of skin between his fingers.
They said it would improve
his writing at school.

Edek howled like a crazy thing.
His mother could still hear
that howling in her mind.
In the dead of night, she could hear it.
She cancelled the operation.

3

'Fish Boy'

There was only one place where
Edek was happy. That was in the sea.

He felt the pull of the tide
when he woke in the morning.

In the evening
he loved to watch the sun set on the waves
when the water glowed with a burning red.

He'd swim all day long if he could.
His body was never tired in the sea.

He pulled his body
through the water brilliantly.
He pushed his webbed fingers together,
making a blade to cut through the water.

His feet kicked with a slick flick.
He rolled easily through the waves.
There was so much power in his long arms.
He was far out to sea in seconds.

Once there, he'd swim with the dolphins.
They'd dance and leap
out of the water around him.

Later, two lads from his new school saw him.
They were walking past on the cliff path.
'It's that weird kid,' they said.
'The one that never speaks.'
'Look at him swim.'
'Look at him dive.'
'He looks more dolphin than human.'

After that day, everyone called him 'Fish Boy'.
Edek didn't care at all.
Dolphins made better friends than humans.
With them he was always happy.

4
Swimming with Dolphins

One day, Edek stayed in the sea all day.
He swam far out with the dolphins.
So far out that the cliff had disappeared.

Once he turned back towards the shore,
but the dolphins surrounded him.
They blocked his way.
He couldn't swim back
even if he had wanted to.

The dolphins led him still further out.
They made strange sounds.
Edek found himself making the same sounds.

He made non-human cries and calls.
Now at last he'd found his own real voice.

Then the dolphins dived down,
deep into the blueness.
Edek followed them without question.
Here there were millions of tiny, silver fish.
Deeper still, strange sea creatures lived.
Some had fins the shape of wings.
Others had bodies you could see through.

Edek's mouth was full of water.
There was almost no air in his lungs.
Any other human would have drowned.
But Edek didn't drown.

5

Lost!

'That boy is always late home,' shouted his dad.
'I'm going to sort him out when he gets back.'

His mother walked out of
the small house alone.
Her heart was heavy.
Her legs felt tired.
Yet on she went.

At last she came to the cliff path.
'Edek,' she called as loudly as she could.
'Edek, where are you?'
She looked far out to sea.
But the sea was empty.

She walked down to the black rocks.
There she stayed all night.

The next day they sent out a search party.
They walked right along the cliff path.
Small boats went out to sea.
Edek's dad walked along the rocky beach
for miles and miles.
But Edek was lost without trace.

Days passed, then weeks.
The weeks turned to months.
Edek's mother couldn't sleep.

At midnight every night
she heard strange sounds.
They were half-human cries and calls.

She was the only person who could hear them.
Edek's dad said she was losing her mind.
Edek's mother knew different.

She was certain that her only son
was calling to her.
She knew he was far away in another world.
Her heart told her that she had to listen.

Months became years.
But midnight was always the same.

6

A Heavy Net

One moonlit night, the sea
was as smooth as glass.
A fishing boat went out of
the harbour far out to sea.

The crew cast their net
over the side of the boat.
When they pulled in the net,
it was very heavy indeed.
'Good catch tonight,' said the captain merrily.
'Maybe it's lots of cod or herrings or bream.'

They pulled and pulled at the net.
Just as it came clear of the water,
the moon went behind a cloud.
It was pitch black.

The fishermen didn't know what they'd caught.
'We'll head for the harbour,' said the captain.
'Then we can see what we've caught.'

After a while they docked.
The boat was moored under the harbour lights.
All eyes peered into the net.
'Looks like a load of seaweed,' said a sailor.
'No fish at all to sell.'

The captain bent down low to look at the net.
'Something's moving in there,' he said.
'Something's alive.'
He put his boot into the net.
He pushed the seaweed back.

Something moved for sure.
It wasn't cod or herrings or even bream,
but the strangest creature he'd ever seen.

'I don't believe it,' said the captain.
'Surely it can't be true.'

The sailors climbed out of the boat.
They ran to the far end of the village.

Edek's dad and mother came running,
back to the harbour wall.

They both knelt down by the net.
Something in the net had a long, stick body.

Edek's mother pressed her hands on the body.
Water gushed out.
She pressed and pressed again.
The stick body came to life.

'It's a miracle,' cried the mother.
'Edek has returned alive.'

7

A Time to Celebrate

They covered Edek in a blanket
and carried him home.
When they were inside the house,
Edek's dad spoke.
'Shut all the windows.
Lock the door.
Don't let him out.'

'Edek shouldn't be a prisoner here,'
said the mother.
'He should be having a party.
The whole village will want a party.
Don't you want to celebrate?
Our lost son has come back to us.'

24

'There'll be no party,' growled the father.
'I'm going to get a new lock.
I'll buy a huge bolt for the door.
He's never going to swim in the sea again.'

The mother took the blanket
gently off her son.
Then she froze.
His skin was covered in scales.
The web between his fingers had grown.
There was a new web on each foot.
He was more fish than ever.

Edek shrank back from her.
'You're still our son,' she said.
Then she cuddled him for hours.

8

The Storm

All day a storm was building.
The sky was black at midday.
A fierce wind howled through the village.
At sea, the waves were taller
than the tallest house.

That night Edek's dad went to the inn.
'Please don't go.
Not tonight,' said Edek's mother.
But he went just the same,
locking the door firmly behind him.
He placed the key in his pocket.
It fitted the huge iron padlock
that he'd newly bought.

In the house, son and mother sat in silence.
Edek's head and eyes
were turned towards the sea,
just as they had been all day.

The wind grew into a storm force gale.
The door rattled and creaked.
Smoke from the fire was blown
back down the chimney.

Then the thunder and lightning began.
Great forks of jagged lightning lit up the sky.
The thunder crashes were deafening.

The storm hit the house in full fury.
There was a massive flash of lightning.

The bolt on the cottage door sprang back,
as the huge iron padlock was broken in half.
The door flew open,
though there was no one near it.

Edek's watery eyes stared out
into the pouring rain –
a boy more fish than human.

He turned to his mother for the last time.
She threw her arms around him
and held him tightly.
She cuddled him for a while,
sobbing the whole time.

Then she opened her arms and let him go.